FOR JUSTIN, JULIE-ANNE, AND JESSICA—A.D.

TO MY BEAUTIFUL WIFE, CLARE—D.M.

Text copyright © 2017 by Anh Do
Illustrations by Dan McGuiness

ISBN 978-1-338-58721-0

10 9 8 7 6 5 4 3 2 1   20 21 22 23 24

Printed in the U.S.A.   23
This edition first printing 2020

Typeset in YWFT Mullino.

ANH DO

ILLUSTRATED BY
DAN McGUINESS

HOT DOG! 2

PARTY TIME!

Scholastic Inc.

ONE

Hi, I'm Hotdog. I'm a wiener dog.
I'm like an ordinary dog that's been
s-t-r-e-t-c-h-e-d.

You must meet my two **best** friends.

There's *Lizzie the Lizard.*

And *Kev the cat.*

It's Kev's birthday today, and we're throwing him a surprise party at my place!

SHHH! DON'T TELL HIM!

Kev doesn't have a clue! We've been working really hard on our party planning. We have loads of food, games, and other fun things!

We have . . .

lots of sprinkles ready for cookie decorating!

Corn kernels for popcorn!

And a **HUGE** wobbly cake made out of **Jell-Yum gelatin**!

We've chosen some of our favorite games to play . . . like pin the tail on the donkey.

Kev really likes lollipops, so Lizzie's been working on a huge CHICKEN piñata for him.

A piñata is like a big box made out of paper that you fill with candy. Then you hit it with a stick while wearing a blindfold! And candy rains down!

But what Kev likes most of all . . .
is **dinosaurs**!

I had blown up heaps of **balloons**,
and Lizzie wanted to make them look
like **dinosaurs** by adding **eyes**
and teeth.

ALMOST DONE.

They looked really scary!

"Great job, Lizzie," I said. "Let's hide those away in the closet for now . . ."

Best of all, Lizzie was going to perform some magic!

She'd been practicing her tricks for weeks.

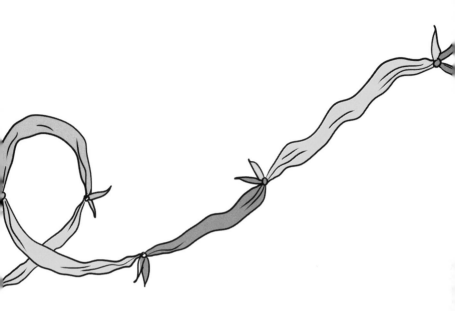

Like the **never-ending hanky!**

She also tried the pulling-a-coin-from-behind-my-ear trick.

EEEK!
HOW OFTEN DO YOU WASH BEHIND YOUR EARS?

ONCE A YEAR, WHETHER I NEED TO OR NOT.

But Lizzie's best trick was . . .

SAWING A
HOTDOG
IN HALF!

Trust me, I was NOT HAPPY about
that one at first!

But once Lizzie explained to me how it would work, I agreed to do it.

For Kev!

He was going to **Love** it!

It had been **REALLY hard** keeping
Kev away from all our party planning.

NOTHING TO
SEE THERE!

Especially today, as it was his birthday, and we hadn't even wished him a happy birthday yet!

In fact, we'd kept him outside all morning.

He was starting to look really sad.
Really, really sad.

That would all change as soon as we crossed off the last thing on our list of things to do.

BUY KEV'S PRESENT!

And we knew exactly what to get him!

TWO

Kev didn't want to stay behind, so we had to take him with us to the store.

On the way, Lizzie leaned over and whispered in my ear, "How are we going to buy his present without him **SEEING**?!"

"What did you say?" asked Kev.

Lizzie's good at making things up, so she told Kev, "Have you ever seen a polar bear PEEING?"

Lizzie and I both laughed.

HA HA HA HA HA!

We'd only taken a few more steps before Lizzie started whispering again.

I don't think Lizzie knows how to whisper properly. She just shouts while covering her mouth.

"Hotdog," she said, "it could ruin the SURPRISE!"

"What did you say?" Kev asked.

Lizzie thought quickly and then told Kev, "Umm, I think I've got something in MY EYES!"

"There sure is something in there . . ." said Kev. "Your eyeballs!"

Kev thought that was a great joke, and we all laughed.

Phew, Kev still had no idea about the party! I left Lizzie outside the store, trying to distract him, while I ran inside to find the ROARING DINO BIKE!

LOOK AT ME, LOOK AT ME, NOTHING TO SEE, LOOK AT MEEEEEE!

There was only one bike left!

SALE!

ARING DINO BIKE!

I grabbed the last one just in time . . .

not knowing that someone else really wanted that bike, too!

I felt a **bit bad** that I'd taken the last bike, but I had **bigger** things to worry about. Like, how to hide the bike and get it home!

"Wow," said Kev. "You must really need toilet paper."

"You never know when you gotta go," I said with a shrug.

Lizzie had something slung over her shoulder.

"What's that?" I asked her.

"Me and Kev found a pair of roller skates in the trash! Someone had thrown them out!"

"What are you going to do with those?"
I asked.

"You never know when you gotta
roll," said Lizzie.

Just as we turned the corner toward my place, I thought I saw something that looked like the rooster and donkey behind us.

But it was just a

funny-looking bush.

Besides, what would they be doing

following

us home?

THREE

Kev was **NOT** happy about waiting outside again.

"We just need you to, um, watch the cart while we take the, um, toilet paper inside," said Lizzie.

"That's right," I agreed. "We won't be long. I promise."

As we carried the box inside, I heard Kev say to himself, "I can't believe my best friends didn't even remember my birthday . . ."

We had to hurry! It was terrible seeing Kev so sad!

Once we were inside, we tied a ribbon around the box. Then we ducked down and hid behind the couch.

"Kev!" I shouted. "You can come in now!"

The door slowly opened, and Kev shuffled in. "Where is everyone?" he grumbled. "Looks like I'm on my own again—"

Kev was **so surprised** he jumped back like a **startled frog**!

"Happy birthday, big guy!" Lizzie sang out.

"**Wow!**" said Kev. "I thought you'd forgotten!"

"We'd **never forget** your birthday," I said, giving Kev a hug.

"**NEVER**, you crazy cat," said Lizzie. "We've been working **FOR DAYS** on making sure you have the **greatest party EVER!**"

"That's right!" I said. "Now let's start with your present!"

"The toilet paper was for me all along?" asked Kev.

"Don't be silly," said Lizzie. "Your present's underneath the toilet paper."

Kev ripped off the **ribbon** and **tore apart the box.**

Kev jumped right on the bike and started zooming around the room. He was popping wheelies, spinning around, and roaring like a T. rex!

ROAR!

It was awesome. Actually, it was
ROARSOME!

"Let me on!" yelled Lizzie.

Kev skidded by, and Lizzie jumped on.
As they zipped away, I thought I saw
the ROOSTER and DONKEY watching
them through the window.

In fact, **I DID** see the **ROOSTER** and **DONKEY** watching through the window.

They had their eyes on Kev's new bike!

And they were trying to get in!

This was meant to be the greatest birthday party ever. I couldn't have one rude rooster and one cranky donkey ruining it! We'd made Kev really sad this morning, so now we had to make it up to him!

Somehow I needed to get rid of those guys without Kev finding out what was going on!

It was going to be one tough mission. But I'm always up for anything!

FOUR

Kev was so happy when he saw his cake! "**Jell-Yum! My favorite!**" he said.

He was so distracted by the wobbling treat that it gave me a chance to pull Lizzie aside.

"Lizzie," I whispered, "we have trouble. Rooster and Donkey are outside. They followed us home from the store. I bought the last bike, and they are NOT HAPPY."

I THINK THEY'RE GOING TO TRY AND STEAL KEV'S BIKE!

Lizzie looked real mad.

"What did you say?" asked Kev.

"Um," said Lizzie, "when it comes to making Jell-Yum, Hotdog's a WIZARD!"

All of a sudden we were interrupted by a loud thud on the roof.

"What was that?" said Kev.

It must have been those pesky guys up there, trying to get in through the chimney!

THUD!
THUD!

I had to **think fast**!

"It must be the, um, **pigeons** back again," I said. "They love hanging out on our roof."

THEY MUST BE SOME BIG PIGEONS!

"HUGE," I said. "They spend a lot of time at the gym working out."

I needed to get Kev away from the fireplace!

"Kev," I said, "why don't you go and help Lizzie cook the popcorn?"

"Ooh, popcorn, my other favorite!"
said Kev.

I watched as Lizzie grabbed the huge
bag of corn kernels . . . and poured the
WHOLE THING into the pot.

THAT
SHOULD
BE
ENOUGH!

I thought it was *waaaaay* too much, but I had bigger things to worry about!

The *thudding* above was getting *louder* ... I was pretty sure *Rooster* and *Donkey* were moments away from landing inside!

I needed to do something!

I grabbed the Jell-Yum and shoved it under the chimney.

I hid **under** the table, waiting for the rooster and donkey to arrive.

The **rooster** landed first.

SPLAT!

Then the **donkey**!

They were both completely **COVERED** in Jell-Yum! It was so funny!

They couldn't even stand up. They kept **slipping** and **falling** over!

"Get up and grab that bike, Donkey!" screeched the rooster to the donkey.

"YOU get up and get it, Rooster!" said the donkey, who was slipping like a giraffe on ice!

Just when I thought it couldn't get any funnier, Rooster fell onto the table . . .

... and emptied the **sprinkles** all over himself and his buddy!

"Let's get out of here!" said Donkey.

Donkey finally climbed to his feet and ran for the nearest door, which was the door to the closet!

It was the closet that was filled with the creepy-looking balloons!

ARGHHHH!

Donkey screamed!

MONSTERS!

"Everything okay in there?" yelled out Lizzie.

I called back—

JUST A LITTLE SPRINKLE SPILL!

I'd stopped Rooster and Donkey from STEALING KEV'S DINO BIKE!

Now it was time for me to get back to the party!

"The rooster and donkey ran away," I whispered to Lizzie.

Now we could get our party games started!

. . . OR SO I THOUGHT!

They hadn't gone anywhere!

I was just getting our **first game** ready when . . .

SCREECH!
ZOOOM!

I turned back around, and
the bike was gone!

SMELL
YOU
LATER!

Kev looked **sadder** than ever!

THEY STOLE MY BIKE?!

"Ooh, they have messed with the **WRONG party!**" said Lizzie.

I couldn't let them get away. I had to come up with an idea to chase them down, **fast!**

"Don't worry, Kev!" I said. "Lizzie, hand me your **skates!**"

FIVE

We were FLYING down the street
after the robbers!

It was SO easy to follow Rooster and Donkey . . . all we had to do was follow the trail of SPRINKLES!

We zipped down the pavement,

skidded around the river,

jumped over a few terrified turtles ...

OOH, THAT WAS CLOSE!

... and we'd almost caught up!

Then I saw our chance. A **BIG** BEND in the road.

I just needed one big push to reach them!

"You can do it, Hotdog!" Kev and Lizzie shouted out.

My legs skated as fast as they possibly could! I HAD to get that bike back for my friend!

We sped up like a race car!

We were **SO** close! Rooster and Donkey were distracted by us, and they didn't see the **TREE STUMP** in front of them.

They hit the stump and went
FLYING through the air. They flipped
and tumbled and landed ...

right in the pond!

This was *our chance* to take back
the bike!

We waved **goodbye** to Rooster and Donkey.

SIX

Once we made it back home . . .

. . . we decided to let the games begin!

Kev was up first for pin the tail on the donkey!

We blindfolded him and spun him around. Then Kev wobbled toward the poster on the wall.

WHOA, WHERE AM I?

Kev pushed the pin **HARD** into the donkey poster.

"Oops," said Kev, after taking off his blindfold. "That's not where a tail goes!"

"My turn!" shouted Lizzie.

We blindfolded Lizzie and spun her around really fast.

Lizzie got her pin in the donkey's arm!

When it was my turn, I pinned the donkey's **foot**!

Oops.

Out of the corner of my eye, I suddenly spotted ROOSTER, crouched behind the couch in the other room!

He was back! I couldn't believe it! And he was staring at the donkey poster on the wall.

"DONKEY?!" I heard Rooster cry. "What have they done to you?!"

From where he was hiding, Rooster
must have thought the donkey on the
poster was his buddy!

"Now let's try the piñata!" said Lizzie.

"Great chicken piñata!" said Kev.

THANKS . . .
NOW LET'S
DESTROY IT!

We blindfolded Kev again and spun him around . . . and he let loose on the chicken!

WHACK!
WHACK!

POW!

"Go, Kev!" cheered Lizzie.

But then, out of the corner of my eye, I spotted DONKEY, crouched behind a chair in the other room!

Donkey was back, too! He was staring at the chicken piñata!

"Rooster?!" he cried. "What have they done to you?!"

From where he was hiding, Donkey must have thought the chicken piñata was his buddy!

Surely that would send him running away!

Kev was WHACKING and BOPPING the piñata so hard that candy started spilling everywhere!

POW!
WHACK!

THIS IS AWESOME!

"And finally, Kev," said Lizzie, "it's time for your BIG BIRTHDAY MAGIC SHOW!"

PREPARE TO
BE AMAZED!

"Assistant," said Lizzie. She was talking to me. "Please join me on the stage of wonder."

Kev was so excited. He LOVED magic tricks.

I ran up to Lizzie and climbed into the box, carefully *tucking* my feet away. The fake feet popped out the other side.

I had a quick look around to see whether I could spot Rooster and Donkey anywhere. But they were nowhere to be found.

The dino bike was still safe.

Had they finally given up and gone away? Surely we'd scared them off!

"Now," said Lizzie, "I will SAW THIS HOTDOG IN HALF!"

Lizzie pulled out her chainsaw.

HAHAHAHA!

Lizzie sawed right through the box, just like we'd practiced.

In moments, the box was in half!

Lizzie pulled the halves apart—me on one side, my fake feet on the other!

It had worked!

Kev cheered louder than I'd ever heard him cheer before.

TA-DA!

"Great job, Lizzie!" said Kev. "Hotdog's now a **HALFDOG!**"

AAAAHH!

WHAT IS GOING ON HERE?!

WHAT KIND OF PARTY IS THIS?!

All of a sudden we heard two **ENORMOUS** screams! One coming from our left, and the other from our right.

Donkey and Rooster ran toward each other from either side of the room. They were screaming and running like crazy, their arms waving wildly in the air.

They ran so hard and so fast that they CRASHED right into each other!

Was this what we needed to FINALLY get rid of them ONCE AND FOR ALL?!

All of a sudden I noticed a weird rattling sound coming from the kitchen. Before I could work out what it was . . .

. . . there was a HUGE EXPLOSION!

KAAA

We'd **completely forgotten** about the **popcorn**! It was flying everywhere!

Rooster and Donkey **BOLTED** out the front door!

FINALLY they'd had enough and run away! Phew.

"See ya," Kev called out. "Wouldn't want to be ya!"

POPCORN, ANYONE?

SEVEN

Kev **LOVED** the popcorn explosion.

"First it rained candy. Then it rained popcorn. You both threw me this party. Now I'll help **CLEAN UP.**"

Kev was amazing!

Before long, he had completely cleaned up the place!

WHAT A GREAT—HIC—BURP—DAY!

Lizzie and I grinned at each other. We were SO happy Kev loved his party, and we were so happy we didn't let ROOSTER and DONKEY ruin his day!

"You guys are the best friends a guy could ever have," said Kev. "Come over here and give me a hug."